I Can Do It!

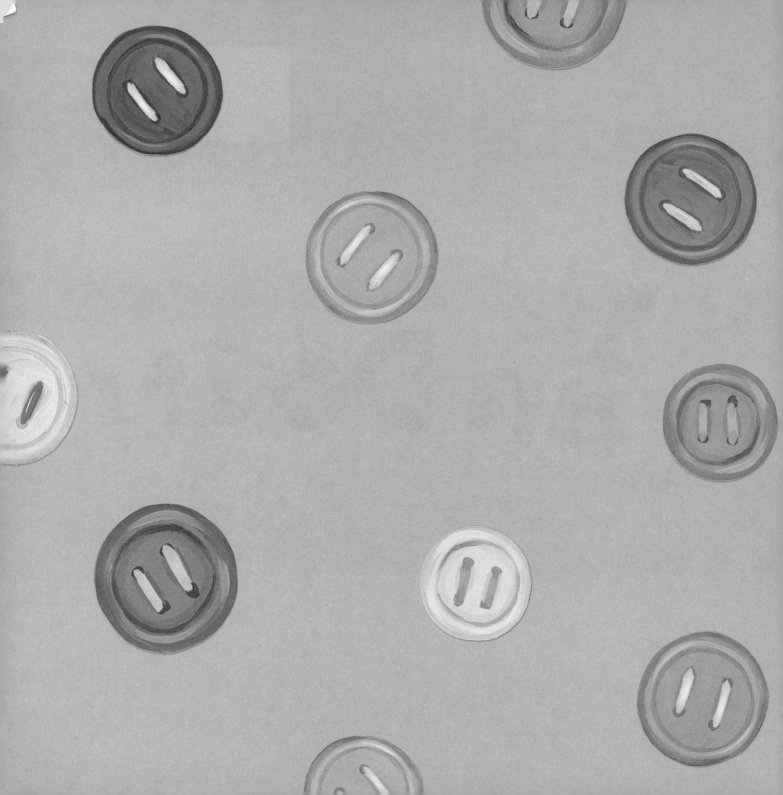

I Can Do It!

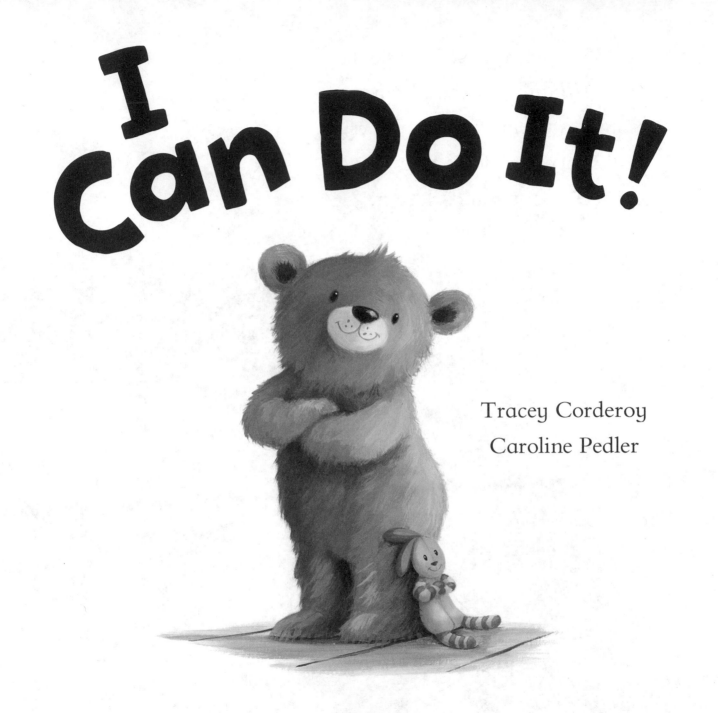

Tracey Corderoy

Caroline Pedler

SCHOLASTIC INC.

Baby Bear had a new backpack. It was *brilliant*, but the big green button was tricky for little paws!

All morning, Baby Bear tried and tried to open and close it.

"Mommy! Look!"
he cried at last.

"I can do it!"

"Clever you!" Mommy said. "Why don't we pop some books in to take back to the library?"

"I can do it!" Baby Bear smiled. And he squeezed *all* the books into his backpack. Every one!

But it was just a bit
too heavy…

Ooops!

Mommy took a few books
out to carry then tried to
help with his coat.

"No, I can do it!"
Baby Bear said.

He wriggled into
it and did up *all*
the buttons!

"Come on,
Barnaby," he said
to his toy bunny.
"Let's go!"

Baby Bear skipped into town
and stopped at the crosswalk.
"I can press the button!"
he said.
But somebody *else*
pressed it first...

"I wanted to do it!" Baby Bear grumbled.

And he plodded on sadly with Mommy.

At the library, Baby Bear raced off to find Barnaby's favorite bunny book. But it was up **very** high.

"Don't worry, Barnaby," Baby Bear said. "I'll get it!"

He stood on tippy-toes, but he couldn't reach.
He hopped and he jumped, but he *still*
couldn't reach.

"Oh no!" said Baby Bear.
He really wanted to get the
book *all by himself*.

So Baby Bear built a big tower of cushions,
and climbed right to the **top**.
    But suddenly the tower
started to sway...

Wibble!

Wobble!

"Oh no!" cried Baby Bear.

And
down he
tumbled ...

...bump!

"Mommy!" he howled, and
Mommy rushed over.

"Oh, Baby Bear!" she said. "You must take care."

"I couldn't reach the story," sniffed Baby Bear.

Mommy gave him a big hug. "You can do *lots* of things by yourself, but when things are a bit too tricky you just need to ask for help."

"OK," Baby Bear nodded.

Mommy helped reach the story.
Baby Bear and Barnaby then turned
the pages and Mommy read the words.
Sometimes having a little bit
of help was fine.

When it was time to go, Baby Bear packed
his backpack and helped Mommy
with her coat.

"I can do it!"
Baby Bear said…

"Thank you, Baby Bear!"
smiled Mommy.
Then Baby Bear skipped
off home, singing...

"*I can do it!* Look at me.
I'm as clever as can be!
But when things are hard to do,
You are there to help me, too.
Now I clap my hands and say…
I can do it! Hip hooray!"

For Isaac, may learning that *you can do it* be great fun! x ~ T C

'If you can dream it, you can do it' *Walt Disney* ~ C P

Originally published in Great Britain in 2014 by Little Tiger Press Ltd

ISBN 978-0-545-80691-6

12 11 10 9 8 7 6 5   19/0

Printed in the U.S.A.   40

First Scholastic printing, September 2014

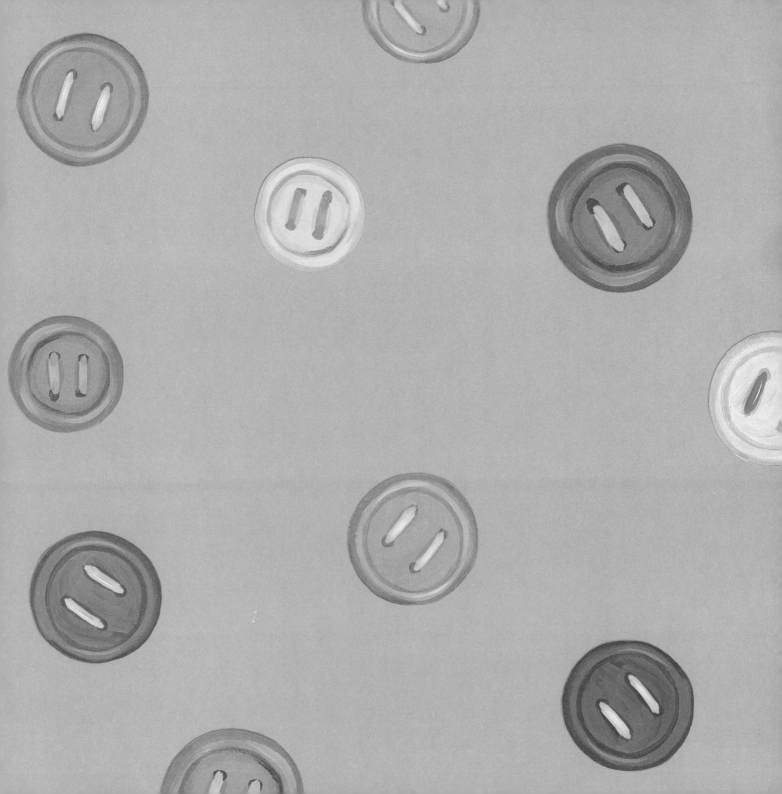